How Long Is Forever?

Kelly Carey

Illustrated by Qing Zhuang

Charlesbridge

Library of Congress Cataloging-in-Publication Data
Names: Carey, Kelly, 1968– author. | Zhuang, Qing (Illustrator), Title:
  How long is forever? / Kelly Carey; illustrated by Qing Zhuang.
Description: Watertown, MA: Charlesbridge, [2020] | Summary:
  "When Mason complains that his grandmother's pie is taking forever
  to bake, his grandfather challenges him to explain how long 'forever'
  really is"—Provided by publisher.
Identifiers: LCCN 2018058509 (print) | LCCN 2019000671 (ebook) |
  ISBN 9781632898418 (ebook) | ISBN 9781632898425 (ebook pdf) |
  ISBN 9781580895781 (reinforced for library use)
Subjects: LCSH: Grandparent and child—Juvenile fiction. |
  Grandfathers—Juvenile fiction. | Time perception—Juvenile fiction. |
  CYAC: Grandparent and child—Fiction. | Grandfathers—Fiction. |
  Time—Fiction.
Classification: LCC PZ7.1.C392 (ebook) | LCC PZ7.1.C392 Ho 2020
  (print) | DDC 813.6 [E]—dc23
LC record available at https://lccn.loc.gov/2018058509

Published by Charlesbridge
85 Main Street, Watertown, MA, 02472
(617) 926-0329 • www.charlesbridge.com

Printed in China
(hc) 10 9 8 7 6 5 4 3 2 1

Illustrations done in watercolor and colored pencils on 140 lb. cotton
  cold press watercolor paper
Display type set in Goudy Sans by Bitstream Inc.
Text type set in Adobe Caslon Pro by Adobe Systems Incorporated
Color separations by Colourscan Print Co Pte Ltd, Singapore
Printed by 1010 Printing International Limited in Huizhou,
  Guangdong, China
Production supervision by Brian G. Walker
Designed by Susan Mallory Sherman and Diane M. Earley

*For my mom, who has believed forever; to Paul, who
gave me forever; and to Patrick, Jill, and Tim, who are
my forever.*—K. C.

*To Grandma, Mom, and Dad, for your patient support.
To David, who bought me blueberry pies for research.
Special thanks to Manhattan Country School for inspiring
the heart of the art.*—Q. Z.

Author's Note

I hope you will discover people and things that you will love forever—as
Mason does in the story. Maybe one of them is blueberry pie. Maybe you
want blueberry pie right now!

    If you don't want to wait forev—umm, a really long time for some
blueberry pie, you can visit **www.kcareywrites.com** for links to easy one-
minute blueberry-cobbler-in-a-mug recipes. You can read *How Long Is
Forever* again while you wait, and dessert will be ready before you finish!

Grandpa's rocker creaked. Mason's foot tapped.
"This is taking forever," Mason whined.

"Do you even know how long forever is?" Grandpa asked.
"Sure," Mason replied.
"Show me," said Grandpa.
Mason looked around.

"Got it," he said. He pulled Grandpa into the barn.
"Forever is how long you've had this tractor,"
Mason announced.

Springs squeaked when Mason sat on the cracked leather
seat. He ran his hand over the prickle of rust on the bumper.
It felt as old as forever.

"Not even close." Grandpa laughed.

Mason stood at the barn door.

"Got it," he said. He pushed Grandpa to the chimney
that reached above the farmhouse roof.

"Forever is how long it took Nana to grow her roses to the
top of the chimney," Mason said.

He traced the flowers until they disappeared in the sunlight.
They towered as tall as forever.

"Nana would be proud that you think her roses are forever,"
said Grandpa. "But Nana knows roses are not forever."

Mason marched down the gravel path and climbed the fence.

"Got it!" he yelled.

"What do you have this time?" asked Grandpa, catching up.

"Forever is how long it takes Mr. Cole to plant his corn." Mason sprinted into the waving cornstalks.

As he disappeared in the shiny leaves, Grandpa and the fence were lost. Mason imagined he was standing in forever.

Then he heard Grandpa chuckle. "Hustle back and try again."

Mason trudged back down the row, took a deep breath, and continued his search.

"Got it," he said. "Forever is how long the water has been racing down the stream."

Mason kicked off his sneakers and let the current dance
around his legs. It pulled and swirled as strong as forever.
"You're getting closer," said Grandpa.
He winked and kept wandering down the path.

Like a hint, Grandpa was leaning against the great elm.

"Got it," Mason said. "Forever is how long the great elm tree has been here."

Mason stretched his arms around the trunk. On the other side, Grandpa did the same. Mason smushed his face into the craggy bark and tickled the tips of Grandpa's fingers.

The tree was old and tall, huge and strong. The tree had to be forever.

"When I was your age," Grandpa recalled, "I could reach my arms all the way around. It's grown so much. But even this tree is not forever."

Mason sank into the roots and leaned against the trunk.

They heard Nana calling them. "It's ready!"
Mason raced down the hill, across the stream,
past the fence, through the shadow of the rose-
covered chimney. Then he bolted by the barn
and up the front porch steps.

By the time Grandpa strolled into the kitchen, Mason
was scraping the last bite of Nana's blueberry pie off his plate.
"First pie of the season," Nana said. "Was it worth
the wait?"
"Uh-huh," Mason mumbled through a mouthful of pie.
"Even though it took forev—I mean, even though it was
a really long wait."

"Would you like another piece?" Nana asked.
"I could eat a hundred pieces!" bragged Mason.
"That might take forever," said Nana.

"No," said Mason. "That's not forever."

Grandpa smirked.
Mason shot out of his chair.
"Got it!" he exclaimed.

"Are you sure?" Grandpa asked.
"Forever is how long I will love Nana's blueberry pie,"
Mason declared.
Grandpa nodded.

"And forever is how long I will love you and Nana,"
Mason said as he crumpled Nana's apron with a hug.

"You figured it out," said Grandpa.

"Did you think it would take me forever?" Mason asked.

An Mei's
Strange and Wondrous Journey

by Stephan Molnar-Fenton

Illustrated by Vivienne Flesher

A DK Ink Book
DK PUBLISHING, INC.

安美

My name is An Mei. It is Chinese
for "beautiful peace."
  I was born on a train as it passed
through a long, dark tunnel.

When the train broke into the light, I saw my mother's face for the first time. Her black eyes sparkled brighter than the sun. And on her blouse was a white swan swimming on a blue lake.

When the train stopped, my mother tucked me inside her coat and we got off. The air was cool and shimmered where it touched the wheels of the train.

We walked down a wide dirt road that twisted and turned as though it couldn't make up its mind which way to go.

Men and women carried straw baskets filled with oranges, chestnuts, mushrooms, eels, and balls of fried rice. A woman was serving a bowl of steaming hot noodles to an old man wearing a big yellow hat.

Cages with small birds were balanced on a rock wall. Little children watched us as we walked by. They were sucking on sticks of sugarcane and roasting sweet potatoes over an upside-down metal can. The flames flickered and snapped like a dragon's tongue.

Without warning, the road ended. A large bird with round golden eyes circled above us. It hooted twice and flew away.

My mother took a small brush from her pocket and painted a red dot on my forehead. The soft bristles of the brush tickled. Then my mother wrapped me in a warm quilted blanket and placed me on the stone steps of the Wuhan orphanage.

I felt her hand touch my cheek before she disappeared. As she walked away, I could hear the wind whip against the metal buttons of her long coat.

I was alone. I closed my eyes and fell asleep.

When I woke up, a woman wearing white was holding me. Her merry eyes danced as she whispered my name. Then she gently placed me in a crib and tucked the four corners of my blanket around me.

The little girl lying beside me was fast asleep, her breathing as regular as the ticktock of a clock.

In the large room there were many cribs, and all the babies were asleep. I listened, but not one moved or made a peep. Then I heard the same sound the wind had made as my mother walked away.

I looked. But it was only the leaves of a bamboo tree brushing against the windowpane.

The days passed. Then weeks and months. Ice drew pictures on the windowpanes, and snow wrapped a blanket around the branches of the bamboo tree.

One day a man with a bushy black beard and skin the color of an oyster shell appeared. He leaned his arms on the rail of my crib and watched me.

Then he picked me up. He held me as if he was afraid I would break, and he smelled of places I had never been. His words were foreign and had no shape.

He rocked me back and forth, back and forth, in his strong arms, and I felt like a small boat on a wide river. I opened my eyes and the man smiled. His black beard fluttered like a crow's feathers. Soon his words became a song. I stopped crying and listened.

Then he wrapped me snugly
in my quilted blanket and
carried me away. I heard a scary
sound and felt the plane rise
into the air, but the man held
me tight and sang to me again.

We crossed water so wide and
blue I thought it would never
end. Day became night. And as
the man fed me milk that was
warm and sweet, I watched his
face. I never blinked—not even
once.

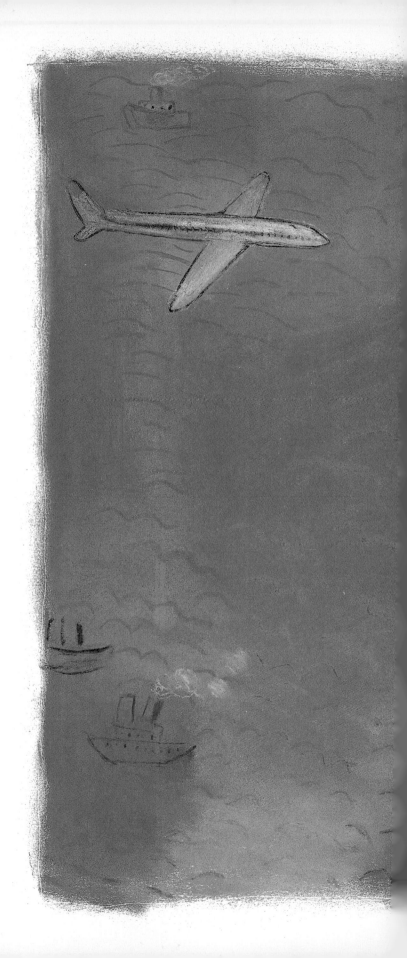

At the end of our journey, a woman with eyes as round and gray as pearls waited for us. She gave us both a great big hug and laughed and cried at the same time. I turned away and watched her from the corner of my eye.

Then they drove me to my new home. The sky was low and dark, and the moon was rising fast. They placed me in a red wooden crib. In the corner sat a soft panda bear. When I squeezed the panda's tummy, music filled the room. Everything looked bright and scary and new.

The man turned on a small yellow light, and the woman folded my blanket over me. I tried to keep my eyes open, but I soon fell asleep.

The days passed. Then weeks and months. I grew and grew and soon learned the names of the things that had once seemed strange and new.

Every morning when I woke, the woman with the gray eyes would hold me and we would sit on the front steps. Flowers as bright as fireworks dotted the trees. Children on their way to school ran by and shouted my name—"Hello, An Mei!"

Every night the man with the black beard would take me for a walk by the river. An old owl perched high in an oak tree made a noise that sounded like Chinese. I wondered if he remembered me. The man named the noisy owl His Royal Emperor.

Then one summer day the woman took me to the park. She lifted me high and placed me on a swing. She smiled, but I turned away.

The swing began to sway. I could see the sky slip and the ground rise. The wind rushed over me. I was falling!

But before I fell all the way, the woman reached out and caught me.

I looked up into her round gray eyes and called her Mommy. Her eyes sparkled brighter than the sun.

On my sixth birthday, my daddy dug a deep, round hole and planted twin bamboo trees. My mother and I stamped down the cool, dark earth with our bare feet. A worm crawled between my toes. And as the sun began to set, we filled the hole with water.

That night a sound woke me up. I jumped out of bed and stood very still. My room was dark except for the puddle of moonlight that spilled across the floor.

I heard the sound the wind had made against the buttons of my mother's coat when she left me on the steps. I called out.

Daddy came in, listened, and pointed. It was only the leaves of the bamboo tree brushing against my windowpane. I climbed into my bed. Daddy turned on the lamp. His black beard was so freckled with white, I whispered that he looked like a panda bear.

When he thought I was asleep, he kissed my forehead, tucked my blanket around me, and turned off the light. Then he tiptoed out. I knew I was safe.

That night I had a dream about a train passing through a long, dark tunnel. At the end of the tunnel was a white swan swimming on a blue lake. It was here that my strange and wondrous journey had begun.

One year to the day after I first met my daughter, An Mei, I began writing this book. This is her story and, in many ways, the story of thousands of other babies from every country in the world who have made the strange and wondrous journey to an adoptive family.

Why do parents put their children up for adoption? There are hundreds of reasons — perhaps as many reasons as there are families. It is not because parents don't love their children; this is usually one of the hardest decisions parents ever make. Sometimes parents realize they are too young, have too many other children, or do not have enough money to care for the baby. Usually their reasons involve wanting a better life for their child than they could provide.

There are special circumstances in China that lead many parents to place their children up for adoption. China has more than one and a half billion people — five times as many as the United States — and if this number keeps growing, soon there may not be enough food or jobs or homes for everyone. In the early 1980s the Chinese government enacted a new law that allows families to have only one child. Many families who find themselves expecting a second child feel they have no choice but to allow that child to be adopted. As conditions in China improve, however, this policy will soften, allowing families greater freedom of choice.

In addition, in China the firstborn son has a special position in the family: He inherits the family property, cares for the parents when they are old, and carries on the family name. This tradition is many centuries old and is only slowly giving way to the idea that daughters are just as special as sons. Some parents, for whom this tradition is still strong, decide to put their first child up for adoption if she is a girl, so that they can try again for a son.

An old Chinese legend says that the dragon takes a thousand shapes and changes color in order to protect its people. Like the dragon, love takes many forms. The red dot on An Mei's forehead is a traditional symbol of love — and it was her mother's prayer that An Mei's journey would lead her to a life of beauty and joy.

Stephen Molzray Fisher